Mom,
The School Flooded

by Ken Rivard
art by Joe Weissmann

annick press
toronto + new york + vancouver

"What did you ▮▮▮▮ school today, Gus?"

"Oh, nothin', Mom."

"Nothing?"

"Weeeell …"

"Why are your shoes and socks and pants all wet, Gus?"

... it kept coming ...

Ms. May said we should
paddle out to the gym ...

The vice-principal was calling his mom, I think, and then ...

"—but there was a LAKE
in the gym and—"

"They opened the doors ... and the whole schoolyard was an OCEAN!"

"Now, Gus, honestly ..."

"You had a fire, too?"

"Not exactly, Mom."

Ms. May said, 'You might say we just completed a science experiment.'

That's when the caretaker came out with a plunger. Glug! Glug! *SWOOSH!* And the water disappeared."

"And what did you do at school today, Mike?"

"Oh, nothin', Mom."

Annick Press Ltd.

We acknowledge the support of the Canada Council for the Arts, the Ontario Arts Council, and the Government of
Canada through the Book Publishing Industry Development Program (BPIDP) for our publishing activities.

CATALOGING IN PUBLICATION

Rivard, Ken, 1947-

    Mom, the school flooded / by Ken Rivard ; art by Joe Weissmann. — Rev. ed.

Originally published: 1996.
ISBN 978-1-55451-096-2 (bound)
ISBN 978-1-55451-095-5 (pbk.)

    I. Weissmann, Joe, 1947- II. Title.

PS8585.I8763M64 2007   jC813'.54   C2007-902352-5

The text was typeset in Myriad Tilt.

Distributed in Canada by:
Firefly Books Ltd.
66 Leek Crescent
Richmond Hill, ON
L4B 1H1

Published in the U.S.A. by:
Annick Press (U.S.) Ltd.
Distributed in the U.S.A. by:
Firefly Books (U.S.) Inc.
P.O. Box 1338
Ellicott Station
Buffalo, NY 14205

Printed in China.

Visit us at: www.annickpress.com

For Keelin, Delaney, Annie, Melissa, Derek, and Erika.
—K.R.

To Murielle, Mathieu, and Judy whose love
and support have kept me afloat.
—J.W.